For Daniel Goldin

First U.S. edition 1998

Library of Congress Cataloging-in-Publication Data
Browne, Anthony.
Willy the dreamer / Anthony Browne.—1st U.S. ed.
Summary: Willy dreams of being a movie star, a singer, a sumo wrestler,
an artist, a giant, and other vivid and exciting figures.
ISBN 0-7636-0378-3
[1. Chimpanzees—Fiction. 2. Dreams—Fiction.] I. Title.
PZ7.B81984Wfj   1997
[E]—dc21   97-2135

10 9 8 7 6 5 4 3 2 1

Printed in Italy

This book was typeset in Stempel Schneidler Medium.
The pictures were done in watercolor.

Candlewick Press
2067 Massachusetts Avenue
Cambridge, Massachusetts 02140

WILLY THE DREAMER

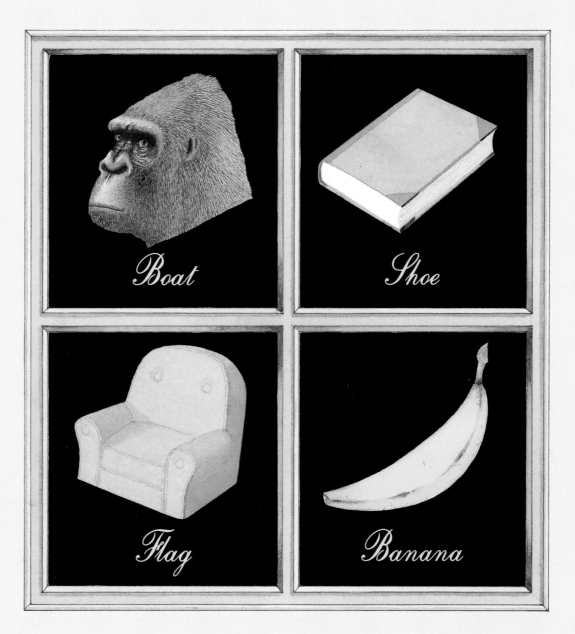

Boat

Shoe

Flag

Banana

Anthony Browne

CANDLEWICK PRESS
CAMBRIDGE, MASSACHUSETTS

Willy dreams.

Sometimes Willy dreams that he's a movie star

or a singer,

a sumo wrestler

or a ballet dancer . . . Willy dreams.

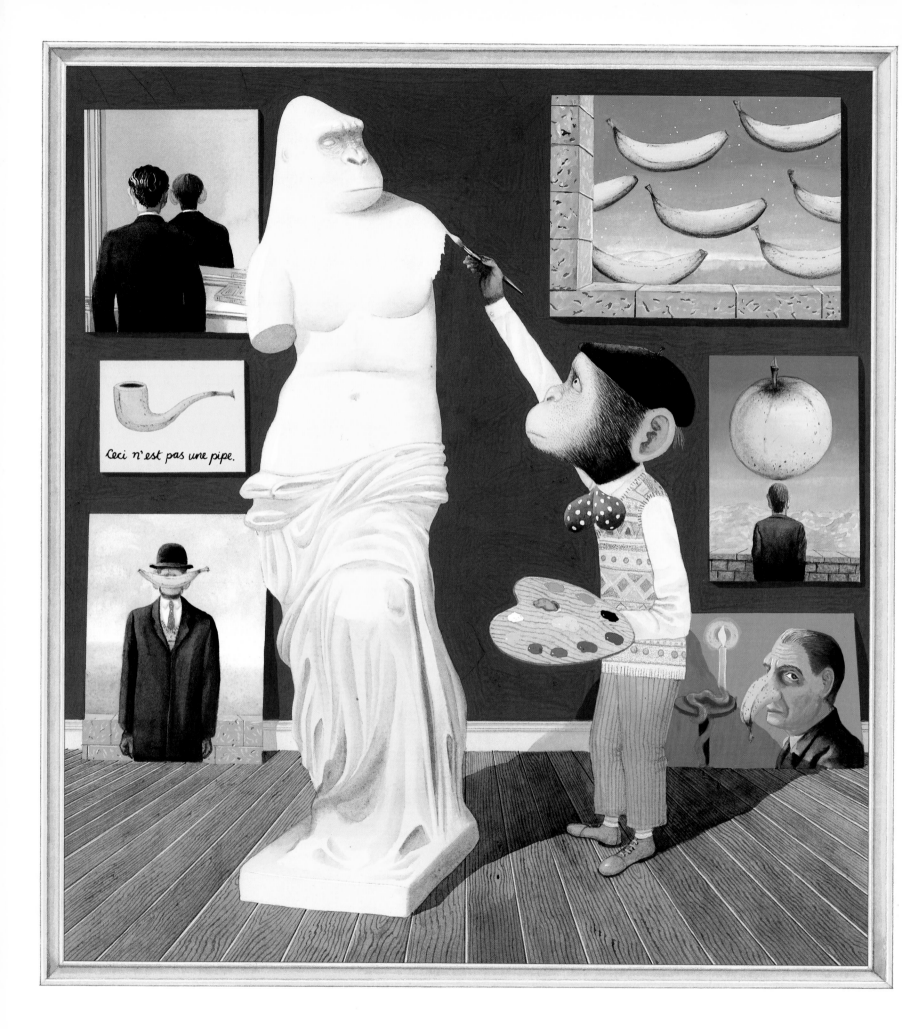

Sometimes Willy dreams that he's a painter

or an explorer,

a famous writer

or a scuba diver . . . Willy dreams.

Sometimes Willy dreams that he can't run

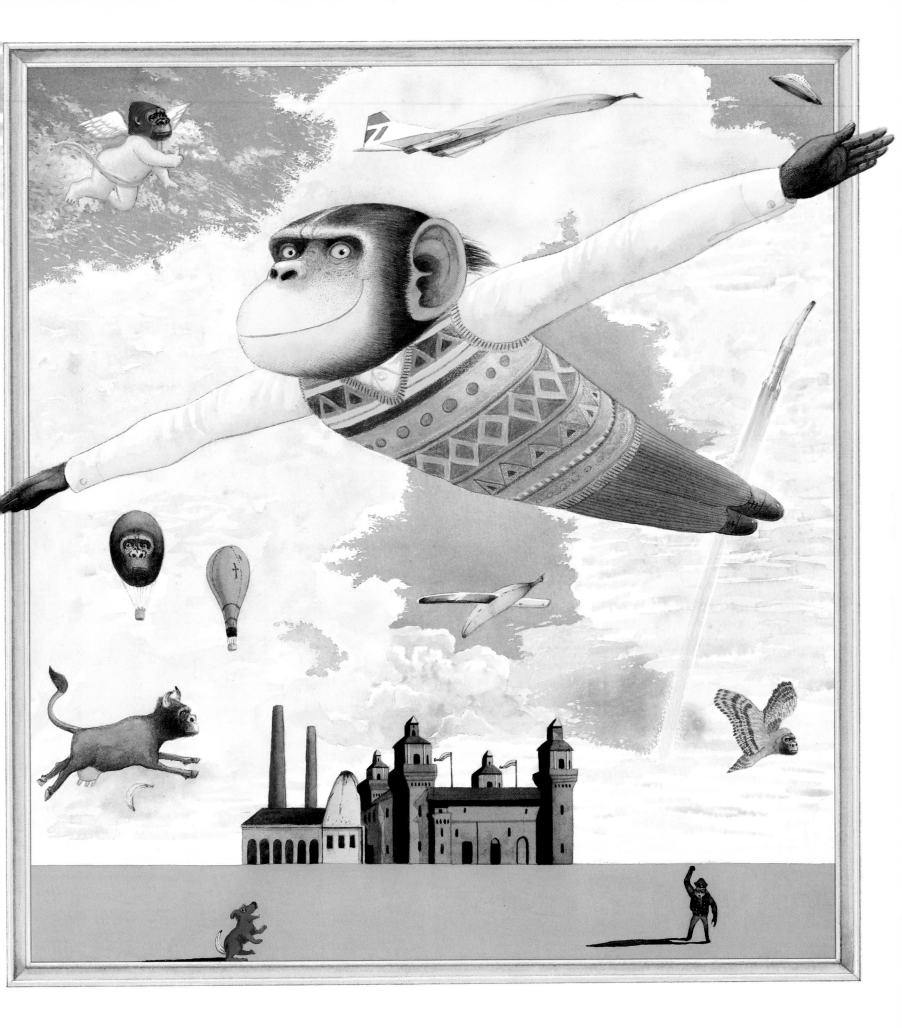

but he can fly.

He's a giant

or he's tiny . . . Willy dreams.

Sometimes Willy dreams that he's a beggar

or a king.

He's in a strange landscape

or out at sea . . . Willy dreams.

Sometimes Willy dreams of fierce monsters

or superheroes.

He dreams of the past

and, sometimes, the future.

Willy dreams.